P9-DCT-920

This book is a work of fiction. Any references to historical events, real people, or real places are used fictitiously. Other names, characters, places, and events are products of the author's imagination, and any resemblance to actual events or places or persons, living or dead, is entirely coincidental.

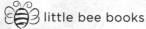 little bee books

An imprint of Bonnier Publishing USA
251 Park Avenue South, New York, NY 10010
Copyright © 2018 by Bonnier Publishing USA
All rights reserved, including the right of reproduction in whole or in part in any form. Little Bee Books is a trademark of Bonnier Publishing USA, and associated colophon is a trademark of Bonnier Publishing USA.

Names: Kent, Jaden, author.
Title: Grumpy goblins / by Jaden Kent; illustrated by Iryna Bodnaruk.
Description: First edition. | New York, NY: Little Bee Books, [2018]
Series: Ella and Owen; #9 | Summary: When Squeaky the gremlin runs off with Owen's favorite book, the dragon twins follow him right into a goblin village. All Owen wants is his book back, but the goblin leader Grom the Terrible wants something else: to battle Owen. Can Owen beat Grom the Terrible in a battle to win back his book and save Ella and Squeaky from the grumpy goblins?—Provided by publisher. | Identifiers: LCCN 2018005685
Subjects: | CYAC: Dragons—Fiction. | Brothers and sisters—Fiction. | Twins—Fiction. | Goblins—Fiction. | Books and reading—Fiction. | Humorous stories. | BISAC: JUVENILE FICTION / Animals / Mythical. | JUVENILE FICTION / Humorous Stories. | JUVENILE FICTION / Action & Adventure / General. | Classification: LCC PZ7.1.K509 Gru 2018
DDC [Fic]—dc23 | LC record available at https://lccn.loc.gov/2018005685

Printed in China TPL 0618
ISBN 978-1-4998-0615-1 (hc)
First Edition 10 9 8 7 6 5 4 3 2 1
ISBN 978-1-4998-0614-4 (pb)
First Edition 10 9 8 7 6 5 4 3 2 1

littlebeebooks.com
bonnierpublishingusa.com

ELLA AND OWEN

GRUMPY GOBLINS

by
Jaden Kent

little bee books

illustrated by
Iryna Bodnaruk

TABLE OF CONTENTS

GET THAT GREMLIN!

"He went this way! Come on!" Owen yelled to his twin sister Ella as the two dragons flew through the woods after their new pet gremlin, Squeaky.

Well, it wasn't *exactly* their new pet. Ella and Owen's parents had gotten them a surprise gift—two gremlins that turned into a lot of gremlins when their gremlin friends showed up and nearly destroyed the dragons' home. Ella and Owen had managed to catch and return all the gremlins to the pet shop. Except for Squeaky, who had somehow gotten loose and taken Owen's favorite book with him.

Ella and Owen chased Squeaky through the forest, following his footprints in the soft, muddy ground.

"Yup, he surely went this way," Owen said.

"Can we please just forget the book and go home? I'm tired of chasing gremlins!" Ella pleaded.

She looked over her shoulder. Their home in Dragon Patch was getting farther away with every wing flap. "If we fly much farther ahead, I'll never get back in time for the Dragon Games. How am I supposed to win the Winged Wonders Flying Championship if I'm not even there?"

"Don't worry, Squeaky's got to be just ahead of us," Owen said. "I can smell the stink of his stinky gremlin feet even from here. We'll make it in time for your silly Dragon Games."

"I've been training for a year so I can compete!" Ella said. "I will *not* miss them because of some silly book."

"It's not 'some silly' book! It's my *all-time favorite* book!" Owen said. "*The Adventures of Azerath the Blue Dragon!*"

"But gremlins can't even read!" Ella shouted.

"Their loss!" Owen exclaimed. "It's the best book ever! Azerath flies to the edge of the world and he has to battle the Dark Troll to save the kingdom of—"

"SNORE!" Ella pretended to doze off to interrupt Owen's explanation.

6

"Fine. See if I invite to you Azerath-Con next month," Owen said with a huff. "And I'm a guest of honor!" He flew off to find Squeaky.

Ella sighed and followed him. "Probably the *only* guest," she said under her breath.

Owen folded his wings in and swiftly landed behind a tree.

"The footprints stop here. . . ." he said, concerned.

"Oh well, we lost him!" Ella said. "Time to go home, I guess!"

THUD!
THUD!
THUD!

"Did you hear that?" Owen asked.

"No! I did not hear anything that sounded like an annoying gremlin jumping up and down on your favorite book!" Ella answered.

"Hold on, Azerath! I'm coming to save you!" Owen called out and raced toward the noise.

Deeper into the woods, Squeaky was jumping on Owen's book. He picked it up and shook it in his tiny green hands. He sniffed the book and smiled at it. He bit the cover. "Meena ooga yucky yuck! Blaaaah!" he said.

Nearby, Ella and Owen peeked out from behind a large tree.

"We found Squeaky!" Owen whispered. "He better not eat my book!"

"That's almost too good to hope for," Ella whispered back.

Squeaky held the book like he was going to throw it, then paused. He opened the book and put it on his head like a hat. "Koona keena kee!" Squeaky marched around the clearing like a soldier with a new helmet. "Hut hut hut hut hut, hee hee!" he yelled.

Owen charged out of the woods. "Give me back my book!" he shouted to the book-wearing gremlin.

Squeaky jumped. He hit his head on the branch of a pine tree. The tree shook like a bowl of barking beetlejellies. Owen's book flew off Squeaky's head as the gremlin plopped onto the ground.

"Ouchy ouch ouch ouch!" Squeaky cried. A pinecone fell from the tree and landed right on top of him. Then another. And another. And then dozens more all at once.

Squeaky gathered them by the handful and hurled them at Owen as fast as he could.

BONK!
BINK!
BOINK!

"Ow! Stop! Ow!" Owen tumbled around, trying to swat away the incoming pinecones with his tail. He tripped over a tree root, crashed to the ground, and skidded to a stop in front of Squeaky.

Owen grabbed his book from Squeaky's hands. Squeaky tugged back. Owen tugged harder, and Squeaky tugged even harder.

TUG!

TUUUG!

TUUUUUUG!

SLIP!

"OOPS!"

The book slipped from Owen's claws and right back into the gremlin's hands. Squeaky opened the book and put it on his head again. He ran off into the woods.

"Hehehehehehehehehehehe!" the speedy gremlin giggled.

"That was more fun than watching a troll do math." Ella laughed as she stepped out of her hiding place in the woods.

"I'm glad one of us is having fun," Owen sighed. "I just wish it were me!"

16

Ella and Owen followed the gremlin's muddy tracks into the Valley Without Hills. They came upon a clearing at the end of the valley. A small village of straw huts surrounded a round pen in the center.

"I hope it's an elf village," Owen said. "That would at least make all this chasing worthwhile!"

"Aw, dragon scales. Here we go again with the elves," Ella sighed.

"What?! I love elves!" Owen said.

"Are you forgetting that time they thought we were spies for the dwarves and tried to make us rake leaves for the rest of our lives?" Ella reminded her brother.

"Yeah, but that worked out okay, and besides, they're soooo awesome!" Just the thought made Owen flap his wings together. "I love their pointy ears and their pointy noses and their pointy hats and even their pointy shoes. Pointy-pointy-pointy!"

Owen stopped the moment he saw a goblin shuffle up to a clothesline and hang a tattered shirt between two hats. The goblin had greenish-gray skin, large ears, big feet, and long, thin arms.

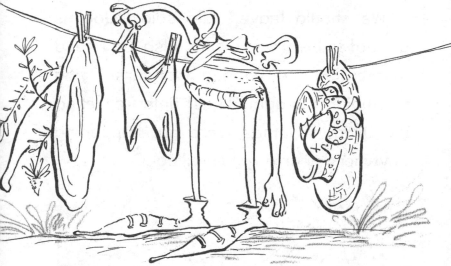

"Hey, what's a goblin doing in an elf village?" Owen asked his sister.

"That's because it's not an elf village. It's a goblin village!" Ella cried, quickly hiding behind a nearby tree.

"Ugh! I do not like goblins!" Owen said, joining his sister. "I don't like their goblin ears or their goblin noses or their goblin hats . . . but I do like their pointy goblin shoes. Those totally rock."

"We should leave," Ella said. "Goblins are not to be messed with. Also, do I need to mention the Winged Wonders Flying Championship again? Last time I checked, the Dragon Games were not happening anywhere near a goblin village!"

"Ah, but do you know what *is* happening now in a goblin village? A gremlin is using my favorite book as a hat, and I'm not leaving without it!" Owen replied.

"I'll buy you a new hat when we get home," Ella said.

"I don't want a hat! I want my book!" Owen replied.

"Fine! Then I'll buy you a hat that you can read!" Ella said. "Let's get out of here before any goblins see us! They hate dragons!"

Ella pulled on Owen's tail, but froze.

Another goblin was approaching their hiding spot. The goblin sniffed the air.

"She can smell us!" Owen whispered.

"More like she can smell you!" Ella whispered back. She sniffed the air too. "Phew! When was the last time you took a bath?"

"Today!"

"No wonder you smell," Ella said.

Ella and Owen ducked underneath the clothesline and ran behind a goblin hut. "Maybe she won't smell you here." Ella choked. "But I still can. Is that . . . lemon? Pee-yew!"

"**G**rella smells 'um a smelly fella," the goblin said. She sniffed the air and crept closer to the hut Ella and Owen were hiding behind.

"What are we going to do?" Owen whispered.

"Grella smells a thing or two. . . ." the creature continued. "Stink 'um stink . . . like . . . *dragons*!"

"I've got an idea," Ella whispered. She grabbed the two goblin hats from the clothesline.

"N-n-now is not the time for shopping!"
Owen stammered.

"We can fool the goblin," Ella explained.
"Goblins aren't much smarter than trolls."

Ella slapped one of the hats on Owen
and placed the other atop her head. Owen
grabbed some straw from the hut's roof.
He spat into his hand and used it to stick
the straw above his nose like a mustache.

Ella did the same. And just in time too as Grella peeked around the back of the hut and saw them.

"Who is 'um you?" Grella asked. "And, uh, *what* is 'um you?"

"We're, uh, gremlin catchers. . . ." Ella replied.

"And *n-not* dragons," Owen added. "Not at all. We have mustaches. See?"

Grella sniffed them. "You smell 'um like dragons."

"Oh, I can explain that!" Owen adjusted his straw mustache. "See, there was a stinky dragon named Ella that flew past us. Very stinky she was. Pee-yew!"

"And then a dragon named Owen, who smelled like a troll burp, tried to talk to us," Ella added.

"But then that smelly Ella came back and she said, 'Oh, look at me! I'm the dumbest dragon in the whole world and my face looks like a Cyclops armpit!'" Owen said with a laugh.

Ella snorted. A puff of steam came out of her nostrils. "And then that stinky Owen landed next to us and said, 'Duh. My name's Owen. Duh. My head's full of nothing but beetle legs,'" Ella said.

"Owen did not say that," Owen said.

"I was standing right there," Ella said. "Also, he smelled awful."

"I did not," Owen said, but then remembered that he wasn't supposed to be Owen. "I mean, stinky Owen wasn't stinky at all. But stinky Ella was *really* stinky!"

"No, she wasn't," Ella replied. "It was stinky Owen!"

"Stinky Ella!" Owen said.

"Stinky Owen!" Ella said.

Grella pushed Owen and Ella forward. "I don't care who smelt 'um worse! Come on! We're going to meet 'um Grom the Terrible," Grella said.

GULP! Ella and Owen both swallowed hard.

"Let's hope 'Grom the Terrible' means Grom's really terrible at checkers," Owen whispered to Ella.

"**Y**UCK! On second thought, they must call him Grom the Terrible because of how terrible he smells." Ella pinched her snout.

Grom the Terrible was the goblin king. He was twice the size of the other goblins and packed full of muscles. He was sitting on a goblin throne made of fish bones.

Squeaky stood in front of him with *The Adventures of Azerath the Blue Dragon* still in his hands.

"The good news is we found my book!"
Owen said.

Squeaky handed Owen's book to
Grom. Grom examined it and then
tossed Squeaky a small cracker in return.
Squeaky crunched it happily.

Grom ran his claws over the book's
cover and bit it, trying to figure out the
book's purpose. Still confused, Grom
sniffed the pages, then licked them.

"Ewww! As if having gremlin drool on my book wasn't bad enough!" Owen groaned. "Please don't eat it! Please don't eat it! Please don't eat it!"

Grom opened his mouth to eat the book . . . but Squeaky snatched the book away, making Grom even grumpier. The goblin king grabbed Squeaky by one of his legs and held him over his open mouth.

Squeaky was about to become Grom's next lunch! Thinking fast, the gremlin quickly opened the book and put it on Grom's head like a hat.

Grom's anger suddenly melted away. He dropped Squeaky and clapped his hairy hands. Happy with his fancy new hat, Grom tossed the gremlin a stinky fish in exchange.

"He traded my favorite book for . . . a stinky fish?!" Owen couldn't believe it!

"I read part of that book," Ella said. "If you ask me, the goblin got ripped off."

39

Grella pushed Owen and Ella forward. "Grom time!"

"Who is you?" Grom asked the two disguised dragons. "And what is you?"

"We're, uh, gremlin catchers. . . ." Ella replied.

"And *n-not* dragons," Owen added.

Grom sniffed them. "Huh. You *smell* 'um like dragons."

"Long story. Troll burps. Stinky dragon named Owen. Duh, duh, duh," Ella said. "So we'll just be moving along now to go catch some gremlins!"

But before Ella and Owen could make their escape, Squeaky scampered over to them and sniffed.

A nervous Ella shooed him away with her tail. "Scat, you little pest!"

Squeaky's eyes went wide. "Meena manna moona!" Squeaky shouted.

"Uh-oh. He knows it's us!" Owen whispered to Ella.

Squeaky hopped around, pretending to be a dragon. He flapped his arms like wings and roared.

"Ooo! I know! You trying to be 'um roaring rabbit!" Grom guessed.

A frustrated Squeaky pulled off Ella and Owen's disguises.

43

Grom stood from his throne and shouted, "Kittens!"

Grella whispered something to Grom.

"You sure?" Grom asked.

Grella nodded.

"DRAGONS!" Grom shouted.

"**I**nto cage you go 'um!" Grella pushed Ella and Owen into a cell with bars.

"And here's 'um your little friend!" Grom tossed in Squeaky and slammed the gate shut behind them.

"Matta paa! Meeta moo mop mop!" Squeaky protested.

"Why're you throwing *him* in here with us?" Owen asked.

"Because he thought 'um you were roaring rabbits! That one dumb gremlin." Grom adjusted the book on his head and happily strolled away with Grella.

"You know, I *never* get thrown in cages when I'm not with you!" Ella said to Owen and slapped her tail on the ground. "And nothing ever wants to eat me or chase me or zap me with a magic wand!"

She scratched the scales behind one of her ears with her claw as she examined the cage.

Ella blew fire at the cage, but it wasn't hot enough to melt the bars.

"Dragon scales!" Ella huffed. "How am I gonna get to the Dragon Games and compete in the Winged Wonders Flying Championship if I'm stuck in a cage?!"

"The flying championship?" Owen asked. "You should be worried the goblins are gonna have a *frying* championship with us as the main course!"

"Meeme mamaa papaa!" Squeaky interrupted. He stuck a claw into the cage door's lock and wiggled it around.

CLICK!

The lock sprung and their prison gate swung open.

"Ta-daaaaaaaaaa!" Squeaky proudly announced with a bow.

"Looks like this little guy can do more than just make us miserable!" Ella stepped toward the exit.

Owen stuck out a wing and blocked her. "Wait a second. Why's he helping us? Squeaky's thrown slugs, pinecones, mud, and cheese at us. He's stolen from us, chased us, trapped us, tricked us, annoyed us, bit us, and hurt us. But the one thing he's never done before is help us. So why now?"

"Because Grom made the biggest mistake ever," Ella said.

"And what was that? Using a book as a hat?" Owen asked.

"No. Annoying a gremlin!" Ella smiled.

The dragons unfolded their wings, eager to fly away from the village and never look back.

"I can't believe after all this I'm leaving my book behind," Owen sighed.

"Maata moo!" Squeaky squealed, suddenly racing away from the twins.

"This is not going to end well!" Ella warned.

Seconds later, Squeaky came racing back holding the book over his head. "Hehehehehehehe!" he giggled madly.

"Hey, he's got my book!" Owen gasped.

"And he's also got every goblin in the village chasing after him!" Ella shouted as she pointed in the direction the gremlin had run from.

Grom, Grella, and a pack of goblins were charging right at them.

Owen flew over to grab the gremlin from harm, but Grom snatched Squeaky up first.

Grella threw a net at Ella and Owen. "Back into the cage 'um you go!"

Ella and Owen ducked and shot up into the sky, barely avoiding capture!

"We can't leave Squeaky behind!" Owen called to his sister as she zoomed toward the clouds.

"You got us into trouble because you wanted your book and now you're gonna get us into even more trouble because you miss your pet gremlin?!" Ella called back.

"But he freed us from the cage!" Owen reminded her, turning around to fly back to the goblins. "I mean, sure he got us put in the cage in the first place, but we can't just leave him with grumpy goblins!"

"Ogre warts! I hate it when you're right!" Ella growled and dove back to the village with her brother.

GRUMPY GROM

Ella and Owen landed at the foot of Grom's throne.

"Why you 'um come back?" Grom asked. "You miss goblin cage? 'Cause we 'um happy to put 'um you back in it."

Owen looked to Ella and gave her a hopeful smile.

"Oh, no. This was *your* scale-brained idea," Ella said. "You tell him."

"Uh, hello, Mr. Grom," Owen began. "We've come back to get Squeaky . . . and my book!" he said in a shaky voice. "And we're not leaving without both of them!"

"And can we please hurry it up?" Ella added. "I need to get to a flying championship."

"Did you say *frying* championship? Because that 'um sounds yummy!" Grom licked his green lips.

"Uh, speaking of frying things, where is Squeaky?" a worried Owen asked.

"Him? He 'um my new back scratcher." Grom reached behind him and picked up Squeaky by the feet before using the gremlin to scratch his back.

"Hey! That's not very nice!" Owen exclaimed. "Let him go!"

Grom growled and gave Owen a grumpy look.

Owen folded his wings. "Pretty please?" he squeaked.

"Okay. You can have 'em back 'um," Grom said.

"Wow, that was a lot easier than I thought it would be," Owen said.

"But you gotta battle me 'um to get 'em," Grom said with a hearty laugh.

"And now it's a lot worse than I thought it would be," Owen whimpered.

"No problem," Ella said. "Oh, Grom? My beetle-brained brother'll go train for a few years and then we'll come right back to fight. Promise!" Ella grabbed Owen and pulled him away from Grom.

"No! Ugly dragon battle 'um me now!" Grom growled.

"Hey! Who're you calling ugly?" Owen asked.

"YOU!" Grom roared.

"Okay. I've got no problem with that," Owen whimpered.

"Mighty King Grom, please let me fight 'um ugly dragon for you," Grella said. "I'll make 'um you even better hat from his wings."

Owen quickly folded up his wings and hid behind Ella. "I'd rather they stay on my back, thank you very much!" Owen said meekly.

"He tried to take 'um my new back scratcher *and* my new hat!" Grom grumbled. "I gonna fight 'um!"

"But—" Grella's protest was cut off by Grom's growl.

"Why do I have to battle Grom?!" Owen asked, turning to Ella. "I can't even battle a plate of vegetables!"

"It's your book," Ella replied. "And your pet gremlin. And you're the 'ugly dragon.' And—"

"Okay, okay. I get it," Owen sighed.

Grom the Terrible stood in the goblin battle ring and chose his weapon. He passed on the spears and the swords, and the axes and the war hammers. Grom chose his favorite: a giant club covered in spikes longer than a witch's nose.

Grom pointed to Owen. "You pick weapon now."

"I can't pick one of those," Owen said. "I don't like weapons of any kind."

"Good," Grom said. "Easy fight for Grom then."

Ella and Squeaky stood on the opposite side of the ring with Owen.

"How am I gonna beat a goblin king?!" Owen was so scared that his wings were shaking. "Even his muscles have muscles!"

"You got this, Bro!" Ella replied, trying to hide how nervous she was. "Just don't let him crush you. Or eat you. Or stomp you. Or smash you. Or—"

"I get it!" Owen huffed.

Surprisingly, Squeaky gave Owen a hug. "Heeta beeta moot moot. Peeta boo moo moo!" he said.

"Wow. What was that all about?" Ella asked.

"I don't speak gremlin, but if you want me to guess, he might've said, 'Thanks for coming back to save me,' or 'You smell like week-old turnip stew,'" Owen explained.

"No more talk! Let battle 'um start!"
Grom roared and flexed his muscles.

"Shouldn't we go over the rules first?" Owen said, peeking out from behind Ella.

"Rules?!" Grom growled.

"You know, like no crushing me. Or eating me. Or stomping me. Or . . ." Owen looked to Ella. "What was the last one again?"

"Smashing you," Ella said.

"Uh-huh. That one," Owen added as he moved nervously into the ring.

Grom lifted his huge, spiked club. "Grom's rules are: I'm gonna crush you! And eat you! And stomp you! And especially SMASH YOU! And then maybe eat you again."

Grom the Terrible roared and charged at Owen, waving his mace in the air.

Ella gasped!
Owen gulped!
Squeaky fainted!

Grom swung his club and missed Owen.

But the effort made Grom lose his balance and he crashed into the wall of the battle ring.

Owen ran to the other side of the ring as Grom got back to his feet.

Grom charged again, even more grumpy than before. The goblin king lifted his club high over his head to smash Owen, but he lost his balance again and tripped, dropping the club.

Owen flew over Grom and accidentally smacked him in the face with his tail. Grom howled with anger!

"Sorry!" Owen yelped.

Grom chased Owen and accidentally stubbed his toe on his club.

"Ow! Ow! Ow!" Grom hopped around on one foot, tripped over his club, and fell face-first onto the ground.

"And that's why we call 'um Grom the Terrible," Grella said with a sigh.

"Because he's terrible at fighting?!" Ella asked.

"Yup. He's the *worst*," Grella admitted. "And if you think 'um he's bad at fighting, you should see 'um play checkers."

"Ugly dragon is too good 'um at fighting," Grom said, holding his throbbing toe. "Ugly dragon wins."

"I do?!" Owen said, peeking out from his hiding place behind the weapons rack. "I mean, of course I do! Because I'm SUPER DRAGON OWEN!"

He ran out into the center of the ring, excited the fight was over, but tripped over Grom's club in the process and crashed to the ground next to Grom.

"And that's why we call him 'Owen the Clumsy,'" Ella laughed.

"**H**ere 'um your hat," Grom sighed and handed Owen his book. "You best 'um warrior Grom ever fought."

"Thanks, Grom!" An upbeat Owen snatched back his book. "Lemme know if you ever want a rematch!"

"Any rematch would be 'um against *me*." Grella glared at Owen.

"On second thought, why fight when we're all such good friends now?" Owen ducked behind Ella.

"That was the best 'um hat I ever had," Grom said. He wiped his snotty nose with his arm and let out a tiny whimper.

Owen looked at his book, then at the sniffling Grom.

"I kinda feel bad taking the hat . . . I mean *book*," Owen said to Ella.

"WHAT?!" Ella couldn't believe her ears. "Couldn't you have decided that before we chased Squeaky, got thrown into a cage, and had to battle a goblin?!"

"I didn't feel that way until now," Owen said defensively. "I've never seen a goblin king cry before."

"You're about to make me cry too!" Ella grumbled.

Owen handed the book back to Grom and the goblin king brightened up.

"You give 'um it to me?" a surprised Grom asked. "Even after I tried 'um to crush you. And eat you. And stomp you. And . . ." Grom looked to Owen. "What 'um was the last one again?"

"Smash me," Owen said.

"Yeah, that one," Grom added.

"I know it sounds crazy, but yeah," Owen said. "But there's one condition! You do not wear the best book ever written as a hat!" Owen said.

Grom opened his mouth.

"Or eat it!" Owen quickly added.

"What good 'um is book, then?" Grom scratched his greenish head.

"I'm glad you asked. Take a seat, king, and prepare to be amazed!" Owen opened the book and started to read. "'Once, long ago, in the land of the Misty Realms, there was born a dragon named Azerath the Blue. . . .'"

"Snails and tails!" Ella snorted smoke from her snout. "This is worse than being stuck in a cage with a gremlin!"

Owen ignored his sister and continued. He read about Azerath the Blue Dragon crossing the Seas of Forgetting, Azerath fighting the Dark Troll and saving Everlon, and about Azerath's courage, his defeats, and his many victories.

"And *that* . . ." Owen said as he closed the cover, "is what you do with a book."

The gathered goblins, who had been silently listening with wide goblin eyes the entire time, let out a long and amazed "Oooooooo . . ."

"Maybe goblins go 'um to Azerath-Con with ugly dragon next month?" Grom asked hopefully.

"Let's not push your luck," Owen replied and handed the book back to Grom.

"Ugly dragon give 'um Grom best book ever, so Grom give 'um ugly dragon something back!" Grom pulled out a box of crackers. "For you! A box of Spider Biscuits to trade for book."

Squeaky danced under the box and tried to grab it.

Ella snagged the box from Grom. "DEAL! Thanks, Grom! See ya later." She pulled Owen away from the village. Squeaky followed them, never taking his eyes off the box. "We've got a flying championship to get to, so let's get flying!"

"So I lost my favorite book that I really did want and ended up with a pet gremlin that I didn't want." Owen couldn't help but laugh as a happy Squeaky hugged his tail.

"That's what you get for trying to teach a goblin how to read," Ella replied. "Now get those wings flapping! I have a flying competition to win!" Ella cheered as the two dragons flew into the sky with Squeaky riding happily on Owen's tail. "Next stop, the Dragon Games!"

Read on for a sneak peek from the
tenth book in the Ella and Owen series!

ELLA AND OWEN

THE DRAGON GAMES!

BOOK 10

by Jaden Kent

illustrated by Iryna Bodnaruk

"I hope there will be elves at this thing," Owen said as he and his twin sister Ella flew through the forest. "I just love elves."

"I know! Stop talking about elves," Ella said. "I don't want to be late for the Dragon Games."

"We have time!" Owen said. "*Plenty* of time! Maybe I can buy a pointy elf hat . . . or pointy elf slippers!"

The two dragons flew through the woods near their home in Dragon Patch.

GONG!

"There's the first gong! The Winged

Wonders Flying Championship is the first competition, and we're going to be late unless you flap a little faster!" Ella said.

"I'm flapping so fast, my scales won't stop clattering together," Owen said. "And I'm all worn out. *And* I'm hungry!"

"We wouldn't have to hurry at all if your pet gremlin hadn't stolen your dumb book—"

"*The Adventures of Azerath the Blue Dragon* is a masterpiece!" Owen interrupted.

Ella continued, "Then traded it to some goblins for a stinky fish!" Ella took a deep breath.

Squeaky ran underneath the twin dragons, scampering over rocks and jumping over fallen trees in the forest. He struggled to keep up. "Huffa huffa puffa," Squeaky huffed.

"Hey, Squeaky's a good pet," Owen said. "Sort of."

"Well, all of his troublemaking nonsense is gonna make me late!" Ella said. "If I miss the first round, I'll be disqualified!"

"Don't worry!" Owen said. "You're still going to be there in time to compete . . . and see your hero, Clara Dragon Coleslaw."

"Xara Claw Wing!" Ella corrected.

"She flew the Pixie Dust 500 in record time last year. She's one of the best Wingers ever!"

"Do you really think you'll get to meet her?" Owen said.

"I'm not only going to meet her," Ella stated boldly, "I'm going to compete against her, and beat her!"

"Well, I'm going to meet some fried pumpkin burgers and *beat* them!" Owen licked his lips with his forked tongue.